Chubby puppies ™

Springtime
in Chubby Town

To Christina, who creates beauty and magic wherever she goes.

ISBN 0-439-35566-4

12 11 10 9 8 7 6 5 4 3 2 1   2 3 4 5 6 7/0

Printed in U.S.A.
First Scholastic printing, March 2002

Written by Olivia Barham
Illustrated by Cary Rillo
Designed by Keirsten Geise

Springtime
in Chubby Town

by Olivia Barham

SCHOLASTIC INC.

New York   Toronto   London   Auckland   Sydney
Mexico City   New Delhi   Hong Kong   Buenos Aires

Peaches yawned and stretched and pulled herself slowly out of bed. She went over to the window. *Another dreary winter day,* she thought as she pulled back the old frayed curtains and looked outside.

But to her surprise, the sky was blue and the birds were singing. And lo and behold, there on the branches of the tree were hundreds of tiny green buds.

"My goodness," she said. "It must be spring! Time for some spring cleaning."

Peaches got to work cleaning her bedroom from top to bottom. She aired out the mattress, vacuumed the floor, and polished the furniture. Then she took down her old frayed curtains.

"I don't need these anymore," she said.

Peaches took the old curtains outside and set them down by the curb for the trash pickup the next day.

At the house next door, Brittany bent down to pick up the newspaper from her front step. As she did so, she spied some colorful things poking out of the grass.

8

She went over to get a closer look, and lo and behold, there under the oak tree, tiny yellow and purple crocuses had begun to grow.

"My goodness," she said. "It must be spring! Time for some spring cleaning."

Brittany cleaned her kitchen. She scrubbed the floor, cleaned out the refrigerator, and wiped the shelves in all of the cupboards. She found an old milk bottle and a large saucepan without a handle.

"Well, I don't need these anymore," she said.

So Brittany took the bottle and the saucepan outside and set them down by the curb for the trash pickup the next day.

Meanwhile, Maggie looked at the calendar on the wall. She put a large cross through yesterday's date, March 20, and said, "March 21. The first day of spring. Oh, my goodness! Time for spring cleaning."

Maggie sorted through all of her belongings. She folded everything neatly in the drawers, paired up all of her shoes, and arranged her hats neatly on the shelves. She found an old canvas bag and a shawl that the moths had chewed a hole in.

"I don't need these anymore," she said.

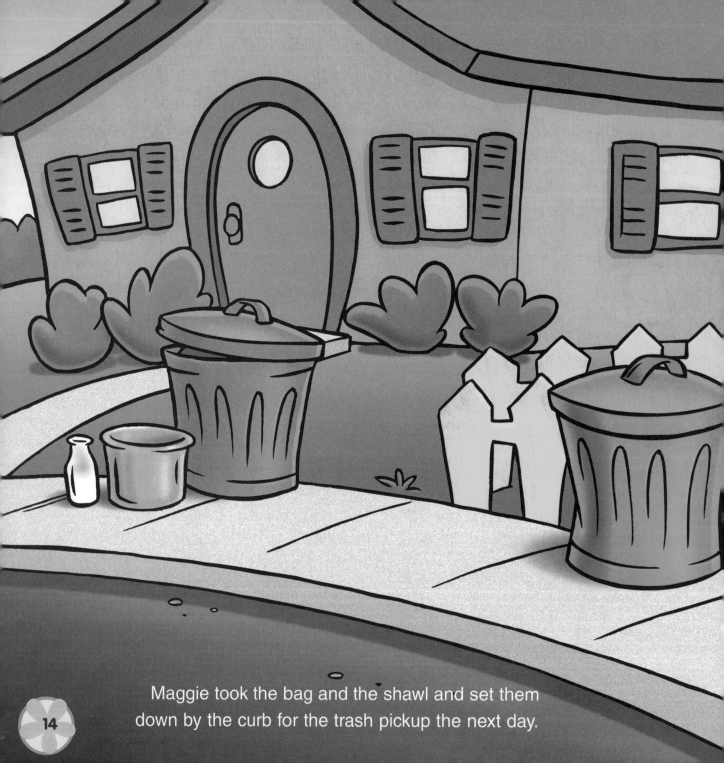

Maggie took the bag and the shawl and set them
down by the curb for the trash pickup the next day.

Sophie went into the shed in her backyard and did what she had done every day for the past three months. She peeked into the box where Tolstoy, her tortoise, was hibernating under some leaves. He had not moved all winter. He was fast asleep and would only wake when it was spring.

Sophie was just about to put the lid back on the box when she saw the leaves rustle. Then the hard tortoise shell pushed up through the leaves and a wrinkly green head slowly peeked out.

"Tolstoy!" Sophie exclaimed. "You've woken up. Oh, my goodness, it must be spring! Time for some spring cleaning!"

Sophie cleaned out the garden shed. She hung up the tools and the gardening shears. She picked up the spilled nails and put them in a jar. She found an old broom with few bristles, a rake with bent prongs, and a picture with a cracked frame.

"I don't need these anymore," she said.

Sophie took the broom, the rake, and the picture and set them down by the curb for the trash pickup the next day.

Max was taking his morning walk. He liked to walk once around Chubby Town every morning for his daily exercise. He sniffed as he walked. Something was different. There was a freshness in the air today.

He stopped to watch the young lambs playing in the field.
That's odd, he thought. *They weren't there yesterday. They must have been born last night.*

"Oh, my goodness!" he said. "It must be spring! Time to do some spring cleaning."

Max decided to give Town Hall a new look for spring. He borrowed a ladder from the fire station, found some old cans of paint in his garage, and set to work painting Town Hall. He had a good time. When he had finished, he looked at the empty paint cans.

"I don't need these anymore," he said.

Max took the paint cans and set them down
by the curb for the trash pickup the next day.

Scarlet sat in her easy chair, in her very clean and tidy house, and listened to the radio.

The announcer said, "Today is the first day of spring!"

"Oh, my goodness!" said Scarlet. "The first day of spring! I wish I could invite all my friends over for tea to celebrate, but my house is just too small. I wish I had an extra room."

Well, it's a shame to waste such a lovely day, she thought. *I think I'll go for a walk.* Scarlet passed Peaches's house and noticed the old curtains by the trash can.

"Hmm . . ." she said. "I think I might be able to use these."

She tucked the curtains under her arm and went on her way down the street.

Scarlet passed by Maggie's house where the bag and the shawl were laying by the curb.

I'm sure I can find a good use for these, she thought.

She draped the shawl over her shoulders and went on her way down the street.

Next Scarlet passed Brittany's house and saw the bottle and the saucepan out by the trash can. *How thoughtful of everyone to leave me all these useful things,* Scarlet thought. And she went on her way down the street.

At Sophie's house Scarlet picked up the broom, the rake, and the picture. Then she saw a bunch of empty paint cans outside Town Hall.

"Oh, I know just what I'll do with those," she said happily, and she hung the paint cans on the broom and rake handles. Although it wasn't easy walking with so many things, Scarlet went on her way down the street.

When she got home Scarlet laid all of her treasures on the front lawn and set to work right away. First she nailed one edge of each curtain to the side of the house. Then she stuck the broom and the rake handles into the ground and attached the ends of the curtains to the tops of each. She stepped back to admire her handiwork.

Then Scarlet placed the paint cans in a circle. She put the saucepan upside down on the ground and laid the picture carefully over it to make a table. Then she draped the shawl over the picture for a tablecloth. She put water and some flowers in the milk bottle and placed it in the center of the table. Then she went inside to make some phone calls.

How grateful all the Chubbies were to be served tea and cookies
after their long day of spring cleaning!

"This is the finest room we've ever had the pleasure of sitting in,"
said Max. "Thank you, Scarlet, for all your hard work."

"Oh, no," said Scarlet. "Thank you. After all, if you hadn't decided to throw away your old things, I wouldn't have been able to build my new room. Now we can all enjoy the spring together."

"Without getting wet!" they added as the drops of the first spring shower began to fall.